The

Wet!
Wet! Wet!

More from the Wizlets:

The Magic Waste-Goat

and coming soon:

Holy Moley!
Flower Power!

The Wizlets

Wet! Wet! Wet!

Jamie Rix

Illustrated by Sue Heap

Scholastic Children's Books,
Commonwealth House, 1–19 New Oxford Street,
London WC1A 1NU, UK
a division of Scholastic Ltd
London ~ New York ~ Toronto ~ Sydney ~ Auckland
Mexico City ~ New Delhi ~ Hong Kong

First published by Scholastic Ltd, 1999

Text copyright © Jamie Rix, 1999
Illustrations copyright © Sue Heap, 1999

ISBN 0 590 11353 4

Typeset by DP Photosetting, Aylesbury, Bucks
Printed by Mackays of Chatham plc, Chatham, Kent

10 9 8 7 6 5 4 3 2 1

To Isabel
A little bit of magic in her own right

CHAPTER ONE

"Brown Owl's A Brown Cow"

It hadn't always been this much fun. There had been a time when Raindrop Henderson had hated the Brownie Guides, but that was back in the bad old days before she found two brownie elves in the forest.

The bad old days had been very bad indeed. Raindrop had joined the 4th Little Piddling Brownie Guide Pack three days after her seventh birthday and had wanted to leave the very same day. She'd hated Brown Owl and the two

1

big, bullying girls in the Fairies, snooty Tati and cold-eyed Priscilla. They'd drawn on her new sweatshirt with biro and tripped her up with the skipping blob. Raindrop had gone home to her mum and said, "Brown Owl's so jelly-wobbling fat she looks like Mrs Blobby. And she's so mean! She made me do all the washing up and clean the chain on her bicycle with my white sock. Look!" Her sock was black and greasy. "And Tati and Priscilla didn't lift a finger. They're spoilt teacher's pets!" But her mum had told her to give the Brownies one more chance.

"Things can only get better," she said. The trouble was, the pack was so tiny – six girls in all – that it was impossible to avoid the taunts and tortures of Tati and Priscilla, and Brown Owl, whom Raindrop had nicknamed Brown Cow, only liked girls who ran around and did things for her. Well, Raindrop was no slave! However things *did* get better when Raindrop was put in a six with the other three girls in the pack and found that she liked them. There was Anita, the world's worst giggler, who had beautiful, black, waist-length hair; Candy, a Kung Fu expert who had a soft spot for puppies; and George (short for Georgina), who was more intelligent than Albert Einstein despite having big bones and being so tall she had to wear her father's trousers. None of them liked Brown Owl, Tati or Priscilla, which gave the four girls something in common. Brown Owl called their six The Trolls.

"But Trolls are ugly," complained Raindrop.

"I know," sneered Brown Owl. "It suits you rather well, trog-face."

It didn't seem fair that Tati and Priscilla were Fairies. Why couldn't the Trolls have a pretty name like that?

"Because The Honourable Tatiana Bortafue-Banks is stinking rich and gives Brown Owl fourteen presents a week," moaned George, bitterly.

"And Priscilla Pinch is writing a book called *Brown Owl – The Most Wonderfully Lovely Person I've Ever Known In The Whole Wide World*," spat Candy. "I wish I could karate-kick her kneecaps!" It was hardly surprising that toadying Tati and lickspittling Priscilla were Brown Owl's favourites.

Then came the day when Raindrop Henderson befriended a pair of brownie elves who were sunbathing on a log in the forest. No bigger than her little finger, she nearly sat on them, but they scampered out of the way just in time, screaming and yelling as if the forest was on fire.

"Duck-down duvets! Watch where you're squatting, you great, huge humphing huwoman!" Their voices were so tiny that Raindrop couldn't hear them, so she made a megaphone out of a bluebell and told them to shout through that. Their names were Shake and Vac and they carried with them a book of magic elfin spells, which they used to make mischief and cause all sorts of trouble for Brown Owl and the Fairies.

"We're the Wizlets. We're wee-widdly wizards," they said.

"You're telling me," laughed Raindrop. "You're widdlier than a widget!"

One day, after the two elves had just turned a drippy chocolate into a spiky beetle on Brown Owl's lips, Raindrop said:

"But I thought brownie elves were meant to be helpful. At least, that's what the Brownie Story tells us."

"We're the black sheep of the family," smirked the saucy sorcerers, "specializing in black magic. We're quite a different kettle of tuna altogether!"

The day the Blacksheep Brownies moved into Raindrop's sock drawer was the day the 4th Little Piddling Brownie Guides started to become a whole heap of fun.

CHAPTER TWO

"Search For A Star"

Little Piddling Parish Council had built a new public swimming pool. In keeping with the rest of the village it was very small, only slightly bigger than a damp sponge, but the Brownie Guides had been asked to perform a synchronized swimming display as the highlight of the opening ceremony.

The pack was in pow-wow to decide who should do what. Their red tin mushroom with the rusty stalk and peely-off paint was broken in two. Its spotted top lay upside down on the ceremonial square of astroturf. At the last meeting, Brown Owl had been sitting on it when the Wizlets had scythed through the stalk with a harvesting spell.

"Any volunteers for the synchronized water ballet?" asked Brown Owl. Six hands shot up. They all loved swimming. "Good, then Tati and Priscilla it is," she said as she unwrapped the gift box of homemade clotted cream fudge on her knee. "Ooh lovely," she drooled, "I shall eat this tonight in the bath, Tati dear. Thank you so much." The Trolls were fed up. The Fairies ALWAYS got chosen to do the fun stuff, and to make matters worse, Tati and Priscilla were pulling faces at the Trolls when Brown Owl wasn't looking. "Now, we also need to think of a celebrity to cut the ribbon," continued Brown Owl, wriggling her huge bottom towards the back

of the kindergarten chair. But the Fairies and the Trolls couldn't agree on who it should be. Candy wanted a kick boxer called Bruce Darm. Anita wanted a giggler like Cilla Black, George wanted someone her own size and chose the Chippendales, Priscilla (the creep!) wanted Brown Owl, because *nobody* would open the pool better (double creep!!), and Tati...

"I think we should ask Prince Charles," said Tati, "because my family knows his family. Very well as it happens."

"You are a clever girl," said Brown Owl admiringly. "The presence of a prince will ensure the event goes swimmingly."

Priscilla neighed with laughter at Brown Owl's sad joke.

"Swimmingly, ha-ha!" she said. "I'm going to mention that gem of a jape in the book what I'm writing about you."

Brown Owl beamed like a fat cat in a mouse house. A tall, thin woman with small round glasses perched on the end of her nose timidly raised her hand. Her name was Sue Slimbottom, but Tati and Priscilla called her Boney Bum. To everyone else she was Tawny Owl.

"Erm . . . Prince Charles won't be able to come. He's in Japan," she whispered apologetically. "I saw it on the News."

"Oh, do stop showing off!" barked Brown Owl. "We knew that, didn't we Fairies?" Tati and Priscilla nodded their empty little heads.

"No they didn't," hissed Shake, who was peering over the top of Raindrop's pocket. "They don't know diddly squiddly, those Fairies. They think a cowpat's something you give a cow when it won't move."

"You mean it isn't?" squeaked Vac. Shake clipped him round the ear.

"You dozy posy!" he glowered.

"Cowpats are for eating, on toast, with chips mayonnaise on the side." Raindrop suddenly had an idea and leapt up off the floor with her arm in the air. Shake and Vac flew out of her pocket and fell to the ground with a clonk.

"Owwwwwww!" they yelled as they bounced on their bonces. "Ironed bedsocks and dressing-gowns!" (These mystic midgets had a queer way of swearing. Anything tidy or clean was used as an insult. Neatness, you see, was a crime in their parallel world, that shadowy other place on the far side of nowhere called Mishmash Major.)

"How about gorgeous Jorg from Hunky Monkey?" said Raindrop. Hunky Monkey was the latest heart-throb boy band and her suggestion was greeted with enthusiastic cheers from the Trolls and a misty-eyed gawp from Tawny Owl.

"You stupid, stupid girl," said Brown Owl. "Absolutely never and not! This is the opening of a swimming pool, not a discotheque. I think I shall ask the vicar to do the honours." The Fairies applauded Brown Owl's wise choice, while Raindrop swallowed her disappointment. Jorg was twenty-one and drop-dead gorgeous. The vicar was ninety-eight and dropped his breakfast down his chin.

"Don't worry," whispered Shake, "Vac and I have got a plan." – which involved a bit of chanting from their spell book.

*"The vicar's the one
Who's the choice of Brown Owl,
Make him come in here now
And throw in the towel."*

The door opened suddenly and, to everyone's surprise, in walked the vicar, wearing a pair of leather trousers, a snakeskin shirt and a curly chest wig. He looked like Gary Glitter in a dog collar.

"Brown Owl," he said. "I've got it!"

"Good heavens, vicar!" she replied. "Whatever do you mean?"

"A celebrity for the blessing of the pool. Let's get gorgeous Jorg from Hunky Monkey. He'd be safe and groovy." Shake and Vac gave Raindrop's fingers a low five, while Brown Owl ate humble pie.

"Well, isn't that a coincidence!" she gasped (changing her tune faster than a jukebox). "Tati, Priscilla and I were just suggesting him, weren't we Fairies?"

"Why yes, Brown Owl, we love him to death," choked the Fairies. It wasn't the lie that stuck in their throats, but the victorious Trolls waggling their told-you-so fingers and tongues behind the vicar's back.

CHAPTER THREE
"Wrinkles"

The 4th Little Piddling Brownie Guide Pack had twenty-four hours to prepare for the grand opening. The Fairies were being insufferably smug and teasing the Trolls about not being chosen to swim for gorgeous Jorg from Hunky Monkey.

"You're too ugly," mocked Tati. "He'd probably think that George was the Loch Ness Monster!"

Candy leapt to her friend's defence.

"Say that again and I'll mash you with

a death grip!" she threatened.

"I'm going to tell Brown Owl of you," sneered Priscilla and she did. Brown Owl was furious with Candy and as a punishment made the Trolls massage her neck and legs until their fingers ached. Then she stood the pack in a Brownie Ring and made an announcement.

"At great personal cost to myself, I have agreed to provide the official finger buffet after the swimming," she declared in a loud, self-important voice.

"Bravo!" cheered the Fairies.

"So I need a detachment of Brownies to spring clean my cottage," she added, looking meaningfully at the Trolls.

"Oh, by the way Brown Owl," chipped in Tati. "I've brought you a jar of that expensive anti-wrinkle cream you wanted, made from the crushed petals of Japanese orchids." Brown Owl was speechless with happiness.

"Oh, Tatiana my dear, you shouldn't have!"

"Oh yes she should," Vac bellowed. "You've got more wrinkles on your face than a worried bloodhound!"

"Calm down!" hissed Shake. "Or you'll fire off a spell by mistake."

"I thought perhaps, as the Fairies are doing the synchronized swimming with me, that Tawny Owl could supervise the Trolls in the scrubbing and polishing of my knick-knacks."

"But that's not fair," protested Candy. "We want to go swimming too."

"Yeah!" shouted Vac, ignoring Shake's warning and boiling over. "They want to go swimming too, you crumpled bloodhound!"

Suddenly, Brown Owl's face transformed into a dog's. The long, saggy nose, the carpet-bag eyes, the drip-drooping jowls of a bloodhound. Shake put his head in his hands.

"Whoops!" grinned Vac. "Accident, honest!" And he cancelled the spell with a blown kiss, but not before a startled Brown Owl had barked.

"Woof, woof!" she said. "Now where were we?"

"Why can't the Fairies dust while we synchronize?" asked George.

"Because I say so," sizzled the old, brown bag. "And you will do as I say, Trolls, or you'll fail your Journey Badges. Understood?" The Trolls understood only too well. It was called blackmail. "And don't forget to lift up the beds when you're hoovering. I shall be checking for dust balls."

CHAPTER FOUR

"The Owl Trap"

The Trolls were steaming mad as they trudged through the village towards Brown Owl's cottage. They'd had a bellyful of that woman bossing them around. It was time to bite back. George kicked a can with a supercharged swing of her size twelve boot. It flew over the nearest house and was reported in Aberdeen as a UFO. Inside Raindrop's coat pocket, the Wizlets sat and sizzled.

"Crisp linen sheets!" thundered Shake.

"Soda-scrubbed potties!" added Vac.

"Pine-fresh drawer liners! That woman makes me mad!"

"Abso – lavender bags – lutely!" agreed Vac. "So what are we going to do to get her?"

"Let's turn her into a real owl," said Shake. "Yeah, one that's afraid of the dark!"

"Yeah. Yeah. Let's give her a moustache," sniggered Vac. "A handlebar moustache with a bicycle attached!"

"Yeah. Yeah. Yeah. And let's enter the bicycle for the Tour de France!"

"YEAH!" They fell into the corners of Raindrop's pocket and kicked their little legs in the air. They could keep themselves amused for hours. Suddenly five huge fingers poked through the cotton roof and scooped them out into the daylight.

"We've been talking," said Raindrop. "George has got a plan."

"Has he?" said Shake.

"I'm a she!" wailed George.

"Ha ha! Got you!" roared the irksome elf. "You fall for it every time." George blushed and lapsed into tongue-tied embarrassment, while Anita got the giggles and nearly choked to death. Fortunately Raindrop could still speak.

"Folklore says that brownie elves help around the house," she said. Shake and Vac could see where this was leading. "So we were wondering if you'd like to cast a magic spell over Brown Owl's cottage to save us all that cleaning?" The wee-widdly wizards considered the offer and then spoke as one.

"No."

"I'll Kung Fu you if you don't," threatened Candy.

"We'll put a snake in your bed if you do," promised Vac, which rather stopped Candy in her tracks.

"But that's not fair," said Raindrop. "Why not?"

"Because we don't do nice magic," they explained. "We've only been taught the naughty stuff." The mention of the word naughty overloaded Tawny Owl's ragged nervous system and reduced her to a shower of shuddering tears. She begged the Trolls to remember the Brownie Promise "to help other people" and not to do anything that might upset Brown Owl. Ever since she'd first seen him on Top of the Pops, Tawny Owl had been hopelessly in love with gorgeous Jorg from Hunky Monkey. She mustn't give Brown Owl an excuse to stop her from meeting him now.

"You don't have to come in if you don't want to," said Candy.

"Then I won't," sniffed Tawny Owl. "Maybe later." She sat by the stream which ran across the bottom of Brown Owl's garden, while the Trolls went inside.

The pay-back plan was simple.

"We set traps!" yelped Vac.

"Yeah, traps!" echoed Shake. "Mousetraps in the bread bin, tin tacks in the bath..."

"And apple pie beds!" jumped in Vac. "Made with real apples – soggy, brown apples with maggots in!" The Trolls couldn't wait to begin. The miniature magicians opened their book of elfin magic and chanted spell number 634, entitled TAKING THE BORING OUT OF CHORING.

"If you have to play the char,
The chances are you're not the Czar,
But housework can be most rewarding,
If it's mayhem what you're ordering."

"Is that it?" asked Raindrop. "Is that all there is to a spell?"

"It's not what it *sounds* like. It's what it *does*," said Shake. There was a glint of mischief in his eye as he showed them what the spell had done. It had polished the wooden floor underneath the hall rug, strung a sticky cat's cradle of spiders' webs across the corridor, balanced a bucket of cold water on top of the open kitchen door, left a rollerskate on the kitchen floor, put a box of freeze-dried coackroaches into the fridge and replumbed the shower into the chimney stack.

"But why?" asked Raindrop.

"Wait till Brown Owl gets home," grinned Shake.

"Yeah!" chortled Vac. "She'll get the biggest surprise of her miserable life." There was a ring at the doorbell.

"Who can that be?" trembled Candy, whose knees turned to jelly in a crisis.

"Perhaps we should go down and see," suggested George.

"What if it's Brown Owl?" sniggered Anita. The thought of Brown Owl

walking into their trap reduced her to instant titter–tears.

"Ssssh! She'll hear us," cautioned Raindrop. The front door clicked open.

"Hello!" called the voice in the hall. "I'm feeling better now. I've come to see how you're getting on."

"Oh no!" grimaced George. "It's Tawny Owl."

"Washable skirting boards!" cursed Shake and Vac. "We must stop her." But it was too late. The prank had already backfired.

Tawny Owl let out a scream as the hall rug slipped out from underneath her feet. She slid along the corridor, bursting through the sticky spiders' webs like a stunt bluebottle crashing through fly-paper. A tiny money spider sat on the end of her nose and waved as she bumped into the kitchen door and the bucket of freezing cold water sploshed over her head. She staggered forward, slipped on the rollerskate and grabbed the handle on the fridge door to stop herself from falling. The fridge light came on as the door swung open, illuminating the box of cockroaches. As their temperature rose, they defrosted, came back to life and dropped out of the fridge on to Tawny Owl's head and shoulders.

She stood up, shrieked, and ran upstairs to wash the filthy beasts out of her hair, but when she turned on the tap, the shower poured soot instead of water. Tawny Owl sat in the bath and wept thick, black tears.

"Sorry," whimpered the Trolls. They were horrified at what they'd done. They liked Tawny Owl. They hadn't wanted to teach her a lesson.

"You were meant to be Brown Owl," trembled Raindrop.

"And I suppose that makes it better, does it?!" roared a fiercely familiar voice from the landing. Brown Owl had come

31

to check on the spring cleaning and had found her precious cottage in a worse mess than it had been on that awful day when a herd of cows had trampled through her sitting-room. Her eyes blazed as she marched Tawny Owl and the Trolls into the garden, where she sat them on a bed of nettles and read the riot act.

The Trolls had shot themselves in the foot. They were banned from the swimming pool. They were forbidden to look at gorgeous Jorg from Hunky Monkey, let alone meet him. They'd be spending all night and all tomorrow morning cleaning and polishing Brown Owl's cottage until it gleamed. After the swimming display the Fairies would take tea with the rock star, while the Trolls would be locked in the cellar. And that, according to Brown Owl Justice, was the last word on that.

CHAPTER FIVE

"Tired Before Bedtime"

The Trolls sent Shake and Vac to Coventry.

"If it hadn't been for your stupid spell we'd've met gorgeous Jorg from Hunky Monkey!" sulked Raindrop.

"And now we won't," glowered Tawny Owl, who had recovered from her ordeal and was just as upset as the next girl.

"Sorry," said the miniature mystics. "Sometimes we don't know the strength of our own sorcery. It can get out of hand."

"But we do have a solution to your problem," twinkled Shake. The Trolls were unimpressed. "We know how you can clean Brown Owl's house and *still* get to do some synchronized swimming and meet gorgeous Jorg from Hunky Monkey," he said cockily.

"And all you need to do is find a rowing boat," added Vac.

"But if you're not interested..." said Shake, affecting an air of indifference, "...well, we'll just disappear." There was a pause. Raindrop was dying to say, "yes, please, we're interested," but she didn't want the elves to think she was grateful. That would just make them more big-headed than they already were. So she said casually, "Oh, I shouldn't go just yet," and then added, "What do we think, Trolls, do we want the Wizlets to disappear?"

"Before we've met gorgeous Jorg from Hunky Monkey?" blurted Candy.

"No way!" Which is exactly what everyone wanted to hear.

Shake and Vac sent the Trolls off to practise their synchronized swimming in the bath.

"But shouldn't we be staying to clear up Brown Owl's house?" asked Anita.

"All taken care of," said Shake. "Brownies, go home! Find a boat and meet us at ten-thirty tomorrow morning, with your costumes on, outside the new swimming pool."

"Trust us!" added Vac, which was easier said than done.

When the girls had gone, Shake became Mr Efficiency himself.

"Spell book," he snapped, clicking his fingers.

"Why do you always get to do the magic?" moaned Vac.

"Because I don't turn Brown Owls into bloodhounds by accident, do I? Quick, hurry, here she comes." Shake and Vac ducked behind a dandelion as Brown Owl marched up the front path swinging two plastic bags. One contained the ingredients for tomorrow's sumptuous finger buffet, while in the other was a startling new flowery dress, bought to impress the vicar.

"I'm home," she boomed. "I hope you wicked girls have finished tidying up!" Her voice bounced around the empty house like a ball in a squash court. "Girls!" Brown Owl raced from room to room like an angry rhinoceros. Her puffy cheeks grew redder and redder as she realized they weren't there. The bath was still full of soot, the kitchen floor was still crawling with cockroaches, and the corridor was still strung up with webbing. She sat down on the stairs and blew a jet of steam out of her ears. Brown Owl was cross.

"Now!" hissed Shake. "It's spell time!" They ran out from behind their dandelion and dashed in through the open door. From where they were standing in the middle of the hall they could see right up Brown Owl's nose. It was hairier than a gorilla's armpit. Shake took a deep breath. This was a tricky spell to chant, because he had to combine two. A spell to make Brown Owl sleepy (Number 4) and a spell to make her leave the back door open overnight (Number 1021).

> *"Oh, eyelids get heavy*
> *And lips start to flubber,*
> *Send Brown Owl to Nodland*
> *(That great lump of blubber).*
> *But as she ascends*
> *The Long Wooden Hill,*
> *Make sure that the back door's*
> *Open."*

"That won't work," complained Vac. "It doesn't rhyme."

"It doesn't have to," replied Shake. "In fact it's better if open–back–door spells don't, because if they do you get weird creatures creeping in and out of your kitchen all night."

"Oh yeah! Like what?" sneered Vac.

"Like 'Clothes Pigs'," said Shake.

"They put muck and mud all over your clean washing... Look!" Brown Owl was yawning. Then she got to her feet, shuffled into the kitchen, opened the back door, switched out the lights and went upstairs to bed.

"See," he grinned. "It did work."

"It still didn't rhyme, though, did it?" muttered Vac, but Shake was already out through the door.

"Come on," he shouted. "Now we've got to change the weather."

Incanting a weather spell is easy peasy for a brownie elf. Shake and Vac learned how to do it in Sprite School when they were still only one hundred and three years old. They stood in Brown Owl's front garden on one leg. Then, having said the magic words –

"The earth is thirsty,
Clouds please bursty!"

– they bent over and waggled their non-standing legs at the sky. Seconds later it was raining cats and dogs. Then they settled down inside a watering can (having first evicted a family of snails) and slept till morning, by which time the rain had done its job.

Chapter six

"Little Piddling's Mighty River"

The following morning the village of Little Piddling was awash; not with excitement as you might imagine (or even with cats and dogs), but with water. It had rained so heavily overnight that the stream, which flowed across Brown Owl's back garden, had swollen to a roaring river.

Tati and Priscilla arrived at nine o'clock to help prepare the finger buffet. They were wearing their laciest frocks and looked like a pair of porcelain china dolls.

"Hello girls," beamed Brown Owl. "You do look pretty."

"So do you," lied Tati, noticing Brown Owl's flashy new dress. It was a dazzling clash of different coloured flowers, which made Brown Owl look like the contents of a compost heap.

"Watch," said Priscilla, raising her right arm above her head at exactly the same time as Tati. "We're synchronizing."

"Good girls," said Brown Owl. "Now come on in and don't mind the spiders' webs. Those dirty Trolls will be here soon to clear up the mess."

But the Trolls weren't coming. They were too busy pestering George's dad to build them a boat out of the junk in his yard. Besides, Shake and Vac were in charge of the cottage cleaning, and now that the Fairies and Brown Owl were indoors they could begin. They clambered out of their watering can, ran across the lawn to the stream (picking up two twigs as they went) and shouted at the water.

> *"Go on river,*
> *Swell some more,*
> *Burst your banks,*
> *Run through that door!"*

The stream began to rise. In half an hour the first dribble of water spilled on to Brown Owl's lawn. Twenty minutes later, thousands of gallons flattened her flower beds and poured through the open back door. There were screams from the kitchen where pinwheel sandwiches were being prepared, then the front door crashed open and Brown Owl, Tati and Priscilla were washed out of the cottage along with the cockroaches, the spiders and the soot spots. Their dresses were ruined. Their hair destroyed. Their arms and faces covered in slurry and sludge!

"Now that's what I call a very thorough spring clean," grinned Vac, dusting off his hands. "What's the time?" It was ten-thirty. Gorgeous Jorg's limousine was due any minute. Shake and Vac jumped astride their twigs and floated with the tide down to the new swimming pool where the Trolls were waiting. Brown Owl and the Fairies, having no time to change and nothing to change into anyway, sat in a muddy puddle, like three drowned poodles, and bawled their thwarted little eyes out.

CHAPTER SEVEN

"Synchronized Swooning"

Gorgeous Jorg from Hunky Monkey was standing by the roadside measuring the height of his wheels to see if his limousine would sink in the lake of floodwater standing between him and the new swimming pool.

"What do you think?" he asked his chauffeur.

"No way, sir," came the reply. "I'm not risking my paintwork in that. I can see the rust worms queuing up from here!"

"OK," said gorgeous Jorg from Hunky Monkey. "Turn the car round and head back to London." Then he muttered to himself, "It's a shame. I was looking forward to the synchronized swimming," and he climbed into the back seat. The chauffeur had just put the car into reverse when a hysterical, high-pitched shrieking made him jump out of his skin. The limousine juddered to a halt as a strange craft made from an old tin bath, several pigs' bladders, a ball of garden twine and a moon bouncer paddled upstream. It was steered by four dewy-eyed Brownies and one slightly older woman who should have known better than to wail and gnash and shriek gorgeous Jorg's name in public.

"Don't go, Jorgy baby!" yelled sappy, happy Tawny Owl. "We've come to save you!"

The Trolls were just in time. Gorgeous Jorg from Hunky Monkey

hopped aboard their leaky vessel and sat down next to Tawny Owl (thereby raising an uncontrollable giggle from Anita) while George and Candy rowed them to the new swimming pool, where the huge crowd (two farmers, one dog and a cow called Myrtle) watched gorgeous Jorg from Hunky Monkey cut the soggy ribbon.

The rest of the village was sitting inside waiting patiently for the synchronized swimming to begin.

"Who's going to do it?" asked Raindrop. "We haven't practised."

"Well, somebody's got to," said Candy. "Gorgeous Jorg from Hunky Monkey's waiting ... look." He waved at Candy from his seat in the balcony and made her toes blush.

"Leave it to the professionals!" chipped in Shake and Vac. "We'll magic up a swimming display the likes of which you've never seen before."

"If you could, that'd be brilliant," beamed Raindrop.

"Go and get changed," instructed Shake. "We'll keep them busy till you get back." Which is exactly what they did. While the Trolls changed into their swimming costumes, the Wizlets summoned a seventy-two piece orchestra out of thin air and sat them on the diving boards to give a sparkling performance of Handel's Water Music. When the girls sheepishly reappeared, Shake and Vac whipped the water into a hundred heavenly fountains that spiralled upwards like columns of twisted ice and descended as fine rain. The sun shone through the roof and stretched a pastel rainbow across the dimpling water. The audience had never seen anything quite so beautiful, and gorgeous Jorg from Hunky Monkey made a note of the effect for his next live concert.

"What do we do now?" hissed Raindrop, as the Trolls lined up along the edge of the pool. The wee-widdly wizards smiled.

"It's a secret," said Shake.

"Jump in and see," grinned Vac. But Raindrop wasn't so sure. What if they'd put an octopus in the water, or a whirlpool? After all, they did only do naughty magic! She looked up nervously at the expectant audience and gorgeous Jorg from Hunky Monkey smiled at her.

"Let's do it," she said carelessly.

"Do what?" said George.

"I don't know," giggled Raindrop, jumping into the water without an idea in her head. The Trolls followed her in and plunged like lead diving boots to the bottom of the pool, but no sooner had their feet touched the tiled floor than they were borne away on the slick shoulders of four silver dolphins. The audience gasped and gorgeous Jorg from

Hunky Monkey whistled wildly as Raindrop, Candy, Anita and George leapt into the *Guinness Book of Records* with a twenty-four hour display of synchronized dolphin riding.

Afterwards, gorgeous Jorg from

Hunky Monkey gave each of the girls an autographed picture of himself. For Tawny Owl he saved a kiss, which knocked her lights out faster than a power cut, and everyone else in Little Piddling got to see the rock star when the Trolls paddled him back through the streets to his limousine. Everyone except Brown Owl and the Fairies of course, who spent the next two weeks in bed, feeding rather nasty head colds with thick, pink medicine that looked like a nosebleed.

Ye olde elfin spelle book of mischeef
and mayhem

For the use of all Humen and Huwomen
of all hues

By His Sorciness The Great Grand Wizard of
Mishmash Major Prestidigitator elect to the
Council of the Black Magic Hula Hoop

This booke belongs to

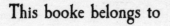

Shake and Vac

If this booke should dare to roam
Smack its bum and send it home.
But if the words should give you lip
Chuck it on a rubbish tip.

"The Acorns"
25 Tree Root Road
Mishmash Major
Little Britain
UnderWorld
Parallel Universe
FIFTH DIMENSION

AUTHOR'S NOTE

The spells wot are contayned in this booke are not very well spelte. We are gud at spelling, but not spellink, if you take our meaning. So pleese make much allowances for the miss-use of sum of the letterings contayned here-in and so on.

The Great Grand Wizard
of Mishmash Major.

YE SPELLES

For Helping The Sickyness On A Coach

This spell does solve all those problems of embarrassment wen you need to be sick on a coach but don't have nowear to put the bits.

Begone quibbling tum and hot sweaty feet,
Wot tells me I'm sick wen I'm on the back seat,
Make me a rucksack with pockets a plenty
For me to chuck up in at speeds over twenty.

Or just take the train

For Livening Up Prairs

Take the boredom out of praying and get on down
to sum funky sounds which will block out the
vicar's dronings.

While everywon else is down on their knees
Plug up my ears with Hunky Mon-keys,
Fill me with joy and make me more merrio
Wire me for sound with a Personal Stereo.

For Making Gurls Throw Like Boyz

This is almost impossible, becoz gurls can't throw like boyz unless they've got a bruther to throw for them, but you can try this spell anyway and you might get lucky.

Curly
Gurlie
Name of Shirley
Make her hurlie
Burly.

Bruthers – don't stand next to your sitser wen she does this won, coz she'll throw you!

For Making Boyz Throw Like Gurls

No spell needed for this won. Just show the boy pigshers of flowerz and ponies while he is growing up and he will throw like a gurl naturally.

For Causing Big Hurt and Maximum Pane To Bruthers And Sitsers

No explanashon needed. This won is a must-do-now for everywon! The best time to cast this spell is wen sed bruther or sitser is occupied on the toilet, for this brings total fun to the spellcaster.

> Yo! Family tease
> Look to your knees.
> Here comes the toll
> There's crabs in the bowl!

Snip snap! Wot's that?

For Turning Plarnts Into Flesh-Eaters

If your Nan or Auntie does have a horrid, yappy
little dog of the rat type, like a Peekingknees or
Chiwa-wa, give her a bunch of daffodils for her
birfday and say this spell. Then sit back and watch
while the pretty flowers make a meal out of Fido.

> Oh buteous bud with petal soft,
> With mouth so fine and sweet,
> Be a flower never more,
> Get a taste for meat.
> Grit your teeth and lick your lips,
> Pets are now ed-able,
> Tell your tum to woof it down,
> There's yap dog on the table!

For Bringing Toys To Life

Ever been stuck for sumthing intressting to do on a boreing Sunday afternoon? Ever wanted to see hoo was the best kick boxer – Barbie or Action Man? Ever wanted to see if your teddy bear could eat six jars of fish paste, twelve cream eggs, and ten peanut butter, Bovril and damson jam sanwidges in one minit without turning green? Ever wanted to transform your clockwork robot into a slave so it would make your bed, tidy your room and do your homewerk for you? Bring your toys to life with this spell and never be bored again!

Fire of life and wind of natter,
Fill my toys with walk and chatter.
Change straw hearts to blood and gore,
Let button-black eyes be dead no more.

Like your mum, only better!

For No Tears Hair Washing

Only cry babies cry wen they get sope in their eyes, but spookily this is the best medicine, becoz tears wash the sope away. Therefore we have a backwards and forwards spell to stop eyes stinging from shampoo.

> Eye sore,
> Baby cry.
> Cry baby
> saw I.

For Getting To Own A Sweet Shop

Don't wait for your pockit money, own your own
sweet shop now, and give yourself tooth holes and
spots wenever you like. Remove your moleskin
trews and hitch a belt loop over your right ear.
Then enchant the lingo as follows...

Sweet swathes of sugar syrups
Sticky sticks of sherbert sips
Sloppy slurps of sucking spangles
Shend my tashte buds flippy flips.

Then replace your trews waistwards and howl like
a dog without a bone. After that whisper the
following in a Cornish accent.

Shops and shelves and entrance bell
Let my teeth go rot in hell.

Then, serve your first customer, close the shop for the afternoon, eat a crate of Chocolate Rainbows and lye down with tummy ake.

Wot we did

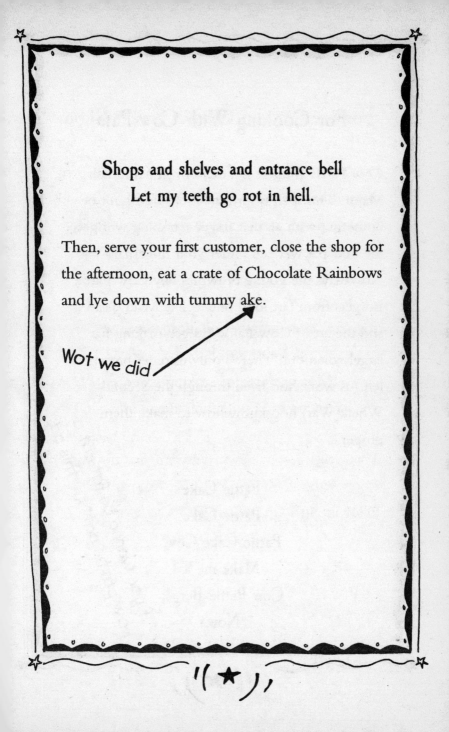

For Cooking With Cow Pats

Cow Pattie Burgers is a delicacy in Mishmash Major. This spell is for lazy cooks hoo can't be bothering with all that finger squishing wot gets the poo-pat wedged under your fingernails. Nowadays the young brownies buy Cow Pattie Burgers from fart food outlets like MacDaisies and the art of Cow Pattie Burger-making has largely died out. There's only us older brownies left (us wons hoo lived through the Second Whelk War) hoo know how to make them proper.

Pattie Cake
Pattie Cake
Pattie Cake Cow.
Make me a
Cow Pattie Burger
Now.

For Fun And Mischeef With Spiders

This spell is best practissed on won's worst emeny or teechers. First you offer the worst emeny or teecher a chocolate (must be a lime cream) and as they put it between their lips you coff loudly and shout.

Spider spider
Born of lime
Give (insert name of worst emeny or teecher)
A hairy time!

For Calling A Bully Names

This is so simple it make me yawn just to tell you. Approach the bully and shout out,

**Bully Beef, Bully Beef, Bully Beef's
A Tea Leaf!**

three times. Then kick him hard in the bottom and run away. Make shore you run fast, becoz this isn't a spell, just a grate way of having fun.

It's better fun to just get a donkey to sit on his hed.

For Creating Beauty Out Of Nuffing

Can't be done without a Hoping Spell. This spell is
not garanteede to werk. We always *hope* it will
create beauty out of nuffing, but sum brownie
elves are so plug ugly it just can't. Their baffness
is beyond a magic cure. The form is as follows.
Cross your fingers behind your back, shut your
eyes as tight as a cat's mouth wot you is trying to
put medicine down, and say this.

> Collieflower ear and broken nose
> Fatty lips and hip-hop toes,
> Wobbly tum and tree-trunk thighs
> Hairless hed and piggy eyes.
> Alter all to make me glow
> With a beauty all shall know.
> But if my fate's to be a hag
> Cover my hed in a paper bag.

Vac!

For Getting Kisses Off the Won You Luv

This spell has come down through thousands of years from the ancient brownies hoo lived in rude huts on Mount Kissmequick. It is one of the Ten Spells of Life and is never broken, although a gurl called Tracey did use it seventy times in fifteen minits at a party and *nerely* broke it. Gurls luv it to deth and boyz go gooey eyed (and stop talking about football for once) wen it's sed to them.

Quixotic
Queenies,
Humbugging
Hunks,
Flitter with
Flutters
And floor-fainting
Flunks.

Fly with
Flirt-flattery,
Swoon with
Sweet-peas,
Plug me
And Hug Me
And Squiddle my
Squeeze.
Nectar me,
Hector me,
Oft
And again,
And Hoover my lips
Till you suck out
My brain.

For Getting Off Skool

In Mishmash Major all young brownies go to Sprite Skool wear they lern spells and magic, so they never want to bunk off. But if they had to lern geography and mathematics, with adriatic equators and all that, I bet there wouldn't be anywon in skool ever. So this spell was thought up for little humen and little huwomen only, and goes exactly like this. Remember to configure the face into a look of horrible pane and tear-jerking sadness or it won't werk.

Mind and body be as won.
I *think* I'm ill
So ill become.

But if your heartless mum is a dragon and don't see the magic and don't believe you's ill and gets you off your deth bed to send you to skool, try this next won.

"(★)'

For Forging Your Mum's Signachure To Get Off Skool

A note for teecher telling her that your Great Uncle Wotsisname has died and you have to go to his funeral is a grate way to get off skool, but the teecher won't believe it's real unless your mum's signachure is on the bottom of the note. This spell turns you into a brilliant forger hoo can copy your mum's writing perfect, right down to her curly q's and lazy r's.

> Oh, spirit of ink,
> And fountain of pen,
> Flow through my fingers
> Afore skool begin.
> Oh, crook of the cosmos
> And villain of the vales
> Teach me to master
> The Art of Tall Tales.

For Making Wind

Like most spells, the Making Wind spell has two uses — won seerius, the other not so seerius, but a lot more funny if made at the breakfast table right underneeth the nose of your grumble guts of a dad. Wind in the seerius sense is good for farmers with windmills wot need driving for to grind the grane. Wind in the not so seerius sense, is wot little humen and little huwomen produce in balloon-sized parcels to make friends sick, and wot cows produce in cloud-fulls to peel paint off airoplanes and melt holes in the ozone layer. This spell does for both.

By the squeak of a cheek
And the parp of a puff,
By the lick of a leak
And the gale of a guff,
By zephyrs and tootles
And rumberling phootles
And silent but dedly northeasties,
By gale force and hail force
And sprouts in baked-bean sauce,
I summon up windy-pop beasties.

Really werks!

''(★)''

For Not Wareing Clothes You Hates

There be a little tailor man, called Geraldo The Goblin, wot lives in the faraway city of Cloth, hoo for a fee of twelf groats and a stick of choclit will slip down the chimnee at night and put his snickety snackety fingernails to work on your worst clothes.

> Mystic tailor,
> Nails so cute,
> Shred my clothes
> To a birthday suit.

Make shore you's not still wareing them clothes when he comes a-shredding!

(★)

For Always Playing Sportz And Never Doing Scummy Homewerk

Observe the cunning werkings of the brownie mind. If all you did at skool was sportz there would be no homewerk. Eureka!

Turn all teechers
Into track-suit preechers,
Let the stud replace the study.
Turn all texts
Into balls and nets,
Let the pupils all get muddy.

For Turning Food You Hate Into Food That Eats Itself

There is an element of preparation before you say this spell. Firstly you will need to decide wot food you absolootly hate. This will probably be marmalade, or cold rice pudding, or kedgeree, or kidneys and hearts and monkey branes and all that yucky INSIDE stuff! Secondly you will need a clean napkin. Thirdly you will need a fast tung to say the spell before your mum or dinner lady stops you. Put the food you hate inside the napkin, hold the napkin above your hed and say very quickly:

Or mushrooms and sheep's eyes

"(★),

Eat me Mr Pastry,
Eat me Mr Fish,
Eat me Mr Pre-Cooked Meal,
And don't forget the dish.

Wen you open your napkin the food will be gone
and your plate will be sparkling cleen like a dog's
been at it.

For Getting Rid Of Parentz

WARNINK! THIS SPELL IS DED SEERIUS!

This spell must only be made under strict supervision. It is *unundoable*! You may think you don't like your parentz now, but tomorrow you might change your mind, and then you can't get them back. Them will be lost for ever in a parellel universe for sinners and football referees. So beware infant spellmaker!

'(★),

Eyes of Mummy,
Nose from both,
Daddy's earlobes
Made of cloth.
Them is both
A part of me,
So ...
Break my heart
And set me free.

P.S. Don't be making this spell anywear nere your parentz or they will be gagging you with brown paper and glue before you've got it done. And we all know what a yucky taste is glue. It tastes like old fish heds. Agreed?

For Billding A Secret Camp

This spell is used by the Brownie Territorial Army wen they play at soldiers at the weekend. This is for sleeping and snoring in woods and fields without getting detected. Another word for it might be camoflarge. You can use it for hiding from the evil bashings wot bruthers and sitsers tell you they're going to do to you, and from mums calling "Yoohoo! Tea's on the table!"

Trees in the sky
And grass on the ground,
Swaddle me high
And gather me round.

For Running As Fast As A Cheater

Running fast is useful in many different situations. Won, of course, is after you have used the Turning Food You Hate Into Food That Eats Itself spell, becoz hooever cooked the meal will try to beat you with a frying pan. You must stand ded still wen you make this spell, becoz speed magic uses gravity to drop into your legs. If you wiggle around, the speed magic will go into your arms or neck or eyeballs (or wotever you're wiggling) and make that bit of your body jiggle like billio instead, and you will breakdance to deth.

> Whizzo me pinwheels,
> Flat out me curls,
> Wind up my wingoes
> And sharpen me whirls.

For Becoming Invisible

This spell cannot be proper written down becoz
the moment it is, it becomes invisible. If I write it
back to frunt it will stick to the page, but it is up
to you to re-arrange the letters if you want to
disappear.

,secaf ywodahS

,sgnut gnirepsihW

raewon ot em daeL

.semoc ydobon raeW

,gniffun ni em kaolC

,edirts ym ecneliS

,ydob ym tuo epiW

.edisni em evael tuB

Wear has Shake gone?